TIME FOR SPRING

BOOKS BY RUTH KRAUSS
ILLUSTRATED BY CROCKETT JOHNSON

The Carrot Seed

The Happy Egg

BOOKS BY CROCKETT JOHNSON

Will Spring Be Early? Or Will Spring Be Late?

HAROLD'S PURPLE CRAYON ADVENTURES

Harold and the Purple Crayon

Harold at the North Pole

Harold's Fairy Tale

Harold's Trip to the Sky

Harold's ABC

Harold's Circus

A Picture for Harold's Room
(An I Can Read Book®)

TIME FOR SPRING
BY CROCKETT JOHNSON

HARPER
An Imprint of HarperCollinsPublishers

Library of Congress catalog card number: 57-5025
ISBN 978-0-06-243033-5

15 16 17 18 19 SCP 10 9 8 7 6 5 4 3 2 1
❖
Originally published by Harper & Brothers in 1957
Revised edition, 2016

TIME FOR SPRING

EVERYBODY said it was time for spring. From the attic, Irene got her bicycle that had three wheels on it and she tested the bell on the handlebar to make sure it was ready to ride. And then, as it so often does when it is time for spring, it snowed.

Everybody said the snow would be gone soon. But, under a chilly gray sky, the snow lay there, covering the buds on the trees and the grass that already had begun to get green. Irene left her bicycle in the house and

went outdoors. She frowned at the snow for a while and then she decided to make a snowman.

"I'll make a very little snowman," she said, because she had very little interest left in things that had to do with winter.

She got a floppy old hat from a pile of old clothes in the cellar. She got three bits of gravel for the buttons of the snowman's coat, two other bits for its eyes, and two short twigs for its eyebrows. She rolled up enough snow for a very little snowman's body, legs, arms, and head. Irene had had a great deal of practice making snowmen all winter.

"This one's very lifelike—for a snowman,"

Irene said as she put on its nose. "Too bad it won't last very long."

"What won't?" said the snowman.

Irene looked around to see who had spoken. Then she looked back at the snowman and her eyes opened wide.

The snowman was fiddling with his nose, pushing it around on his face.

"Can't you put a nose on straight?" he said. "There. That's better now, isn't it?"

Irene didn't think it was a bit better, but she nodded.

"Here's your hat," she said.

"Thank you." The snowman took the hat and put it on his head. "Now what were we talking about? What won't last very long?"

"Winter," said Irene and she made a motion with her arm that took in all the snow around her in a general sort of way. "It's time for spring."

"Ho ho ho!" The snowman laughed a hearty wintry laugh and he gleefully kicked up a spray of snow. "Don't worry about it. Get your sled."

Irene got her sled. With the snowman stomping merrily along beside her, she trudged up the hill.

"About spring," she said, and she hesitated, wondering how to tell the snowman that when spring came he wouldn't be there. "I mean, I'm not worried about it."

"Why should you be?" said the snowman. "Spring won't come, while I'm here."

"What?" Irene stared at him.

"While I'm here, spring won't come."

The snowman picked up the rope that had dropped from Irene's hand and, with a happy grunt, he flung himself on the sled and went coasting down the hill.

"Wait!" Irene slid down the hill after him.

At the bottom the snowman got off and started back up, leaving the sled behind him. Irene went on down to get it.

When she was halfway up again the snowman called to her from the top of the hill.

"Fun, isn't it?"

"I guess so," said Irene, pulling up the sled. "But—"

"Yes, great fun," said the snowman, taking the rope from her as she reached him.

This time Irene got her knees on the back
of the sled and she tried to hold on. But on
the way down the snowman, who was steer-
ing, hit a bump and she fell off. She rolled to
a stop a few feet behind the sled and heard
the snowman's cheery laughter.

"Great, great fun!"

"But I've done so much sledding, all winter long," said Irene.

"And you can do so much more of it," said the snowman, starting up the hill again. "It's going to be such a nice long winter."

Irene picked up the sled rope.

"Do you mean spring really is not going to come because you're here?"

"How can it?" The snowman patted his stomach. "I'm made of snow."

"Yes," said Irene. "I made you."

"Then you know." The snowman continued up the hill.

Irene threw down the rope.

"I'm tired of sledding," she said.

"All right." The snowman turned and rubbed his hands together agreeably. "Let's do something else for a while."

"Do what?" Irene looked over at her

house, wishing it was time for her to be called in for lunch.

"Let's make a snowman," said the snowman.

"No," said Irene.

"Let's build a snowfort and have a snowball fight." The snowman clapped his hands enthusiastically.

"Well, all right," Irene said.

Under the snowman's direction, Irene
rolled snow into blocks and built a snowfort.
When the snowfort was as high as Irene's
chest, which was as high as the snowman's
head, he stopped her.

"That's high enough," he said, getting
behind it. "Now go down the hill and come
up and storm the fort."

Irene sighed and went down the hill where
she made three small snowballs.

"Ready?" she called.

"Ready!" came the snowman's voice from behind the snowfort.

Irene started up the hill, throwing her snowballs. One hit the fort and the other two sailed over it. A remarkably aimed snowball rose over the wall of the fort and hit Irene above the collar of her snowsuit. Cold wet snow trickled down her neck.

Waving her hand, Irene turned and started ‫lking in the other direction.

have to go home to lunch now.”

e’ve hardly begun,” said the snowman, coming out from behind the fort.

“I’ve been snowfighting all winter,” Irene said, continuing on her way toward her house. “Anyway, you won.”

The snowman hurried after her.

"I'll think of something else that will be
fun to do," he said, catching up with Irene as
she reached her front yard. "Hurry up. I'll
wait for you here."

"I'm supposed to eat slow," said Irene,
going up the walk to the house.

At the lunch table everybody talked about the snow and said it was time for spring.

"He says it will stay winter as long as he's here," Irene told them, looking at her plate.

"Who?" they asked.

"A snowman I made." Irene felt sorry because everybody wanted it to be spring.

"Don't worry about it," they told her. "Spring will be here."

They seemed so very sure of it that Irene began to feel sorry for the snowman again.

"How do you know spring will be here?" she asked them.

"It always has come other years," they said.

"I never made a snowman other years, like this one," said Irene.

"Finish your milk," everybody told her.

Irene drank her milk thoughtfully. She got down from the chair and went outside.

The snowman turned and waved as Irene came down the walk.

"I've thought of something," he said, rubbing his hands together excitedly.

"So have I," said Irene. "I think you ought to go away."

"Go where?" the snowman said in surprise.

"To the North Pole or someplace, where it's cold."

"Why?" said the snowman. "It's cold here."

"To be on the safe side," Irene said. "On account of spring."

"We've been all over that." The snowman took Irene's arm. "Stop worrying about me. Let's slide on the pond."

"But if spring comes you can't be here," said Irene, and she was surprised to see the snowman cheerfully nodding agreement.

"Spring, no snowman." He raised one hand, then he raised the other hand. "Snowman, no spring."

"The first part's true," said Irene.

"And the last part follows," said the snowman. "Here we are at the pond. Let's slide."

He scooted toward the small pond and

skimmed across a path of glassy ice that the wind had cleared of snow.

"I've done an awful lot of sliding all winter," said Irene, as she ran a few steps and slid out on the ice.

"And you still need more practice," said the snowman as he watched Irene come to a stop halfway across the pond. "But we'll keep at it, and you'll be as good as I am, along about the Fourth of July."

Suddenly the ice cracked about Irene's feet and she sank to her knees in icy water.

"The pond wasn't frozen!" Irene clambered out and stamped her wet feet. "It's getting too warm!"

"It's getting colder," said the snowman.

He was right. The northeast wind had shifted to the north. Irene shivered and started back to the house. The snowman trotted along beside her, enjoying the cold.

"I don't suppose you'll be allowed out again this afternoon," he said as they reached the gate. "But tomorrow's another day."

"Will you be here?" Irene said, shivering.

"Certainly." The snowman looked at the sky. "It will be great winter weather, too. If

that wind switches back to the northeast
we'll have more snow."

Irene sniffled three times, then she burst
into tears.

"I don't want it to be winter any more!"

The snowman looked at her in amazement.

"You don't like winter?"

"I like it—for a while." Irene spaced her words with sobs. "But now it's time for spring, and I like spring too!"

"You like spring!" The snowman stared in disbelief.

"Yes."

Slowly turning his head, the snowman looked up at the sky, at nothing in particular.

"I understand," he said quietly.

"I don't see how you can, quite." Irene rubbed her tears with the back of her mitten. "About spring, I mean."

"It's why you want me to go away, really, isn't it?" The snowman continued to stare at the sky. "Why didn't you say so?"

"Can't you go to the North Pole," said Irene, "and come back next year?"

"It's a long walk," said the snowman, gaz-

ing into the distance. "Both ways. I'll think about it."

"Goodbye," Irene said, and she started up the walk.

As she opened the front door she looked back. The snowman was still there, thinking about it.

Everybody noticed her wet feet and, because she was sniffling, they quickly got Irene into a hot bath and then to bed. They brought her dinner to her room.

"It may be spring tomorrow," she told them.

"It's time for it," everybody said. "And the wind has shifted all the way around to the southwest."

Next morning they kept Irene in bed to be sure she had no sign of a cold. But by the middle of the afternoon everybody agreed there was no reason to keep her in on such a day.

Irene got dressed and ran to the door.

She looked around outside. All the snow
was gone.

She ran down the walk.

On the grass she found the snowman's
floppy old hat.

"He went away, but he left his hat," Irene

said, picking it up. "I'll save it for him till next year."

Then she ran back to the house and got her bicycle. And she rode up and down the walk ringing the bell on the handlebar, because spring was here.